# Between
# Two Worlds

# Terry Carr

D1363414

THE NESFA PRESS
BOX G, MIT BRANCH P.O.
CAMBRIDGE, MA 02139-0910
1986

FIRST EDITION

LIBRARY OF CONGRESS CATALOG NO. 86-061272

INTERNATIONAL STANDARD BOOK NO.
0-915368-33-1 (REGULAR EDITION)
0-915368-88-9 (SLIPCASED EDITION)

# Copyright Acknowledgments

"Introduction," copyright © 1986 by Terry Carr.

"The Chaser," copyright © 1959 by Terry Carr. Originally published under the name of Carl Brandon.

"A Complete Mystery," copyright © 1965 by Terry Carr. First printed in *The Saint Mystery Magazine*, ed. by Hans Stefan Santesson, July, 1965.

"The Convention That Couldn't Be Killed," copyright © 1986 by Terry Carr. First publication in this form.

"Virra," copyright © 1978 by Mercury Press, Inc. First printed in *Fantasy and Science Fiction*, October, 1978.

"Night of the Living Oldpharts," copyright © 1986 by Terry Carr. First publication in this form.

Dust jacket painting ©1986 by Bob Eggleton

THIS IS A LIMITED EDITION OF 1000, THE FIRST 225 BEING A NUMBERED, SLIPCASED EDITION.

# INTRODUCTION

Some people have trouble figuring out why anyone would continue to be an active fan once he or she has "moved on" to a successful career as a professional in science fiction, and I've had some pretty odd reactions to the fact that I've remained active in both areas. Occasionally another professional will ask me, "How come you're still editing and writing for fanzines when you could be doing it for money?" One of them actually said, "You ought to concentrate on playing with the big boys now."

And the fans are sometimes just as confused. Some of them seem terribly flattered when I write something for their fanzines; and (on the other side of the coin) when I won a Hugo as Best Fan Writer in 1973, there were a few remarks to the effect that I shouldn't have been eligible because I was no longer a fan.

But a fan is simply someone whose hobby is fandom, and how he or she makes a living is beside the point. There have always been professionals who enjoyed fan activity enough to continue it after "turning pro"—for an obvious example, consider Bob Shaw, not to mention Robert Bloch, Wilson

Tucker, or for that matter Jack Gaughan, who in 1967 won Hugos both as Best Professional Artist and Best Fan Artist.

The fan and pro fields have different attractions, so it's not surprising that many people remain active in both. You don't get paid for fan writing, but against the delights of fame and fortune (well, sometimes) you can balance the greater variety of subjects and writing modes that fanzines allow. For one thing, because the fanzine readership is so much smaller than that of professional science fiction, fanzine fans tend to know each other, and their familiarity contributes to making fanzines practically the last bastion of the personal essay. Outside fandom you can seldom publish an article expressing your opinions, no matter how interesting or droll, unless you're an authority on something or other. (And you won't be able to get away with many recognition jokes outside fandom, because very few people are famous enough to be recognized — which is why stand-up comics are still doing impressions of Marilyn Monroe and Humphrey Bogart. The smaller world of fandom paradoxically provides a wider variety of people to lampoon.)

So I write for both pro magazines and fanzines, and *Between Two Worlds* gathers a variety of my endeavors in both areas. They're arranged in chronological order, from 1959 to 1986.

The first piece, "The Chaser," is a fan story that was originally published under the byline "Carl Brandon," the name I use for fannish parodies of famous stories by other people...in this case, John Collier's story of the same title. It follows Collier's plot and style, but its concerns are transposed to fannish ones. On the surface, my purpose was to show that fandom can be considered a microcosm of the whole world; but this rather jejune observation was simply the overlay to the story's satiric point that if fans actually made fandom that important in their lives they'd be pretty ridiculous. (As, in truth, they are at times.)

The second piece, "A Complete Mystery," is also a parody, but it has nothing to do with fandom. It doesn't have anything to do with science fiction, for that matter; it's a mystery story written in the manner of Agatha Christie and it attempts to satirize her Hercule Poirot stories. The satire may be rather broad — I wanted it to be downright silly at times — but it amused Hans Stefan Santesson and he published it in *The Saint Mystery Magazine.*

"The Convention That Couldn't be Killed" represents a type of fan writing in which I've often indulged, so I wanted to include an example here. When you're writing about the fan and pro worlds of science fiction, it isn't necessary to resort to fiction in order to tell funny stories, even silly ones; often all you have to do is write exactly what people said and did, and if you write these anecdotes well enough to capture the mood and tempo of what happened you can end up with a more comedic result than if you'd wracked your brains trying to be witty. "The Convention That Couldn't Be Killed" is a report on some of my experiences at the 1977 world convention; here you'll find famous names and obscure ones, brilliant minds and befogged ones, history with the touch of hysteria that characterizes sf conventions.

In "Virra" we have a serious science fiction story that was published in the 29th Anniversary Issue of *Fantasy and Science Fiction.* If I were to try to tell you in a sentence or two what it's about, you'd be sure I was foisting upon you another silly story or satire or the like, but that's the way science fiction sometimes works. (Go ahead, *try* to tell me in one or two sentences the plot of *Ringworld* or *Valis* or *Neuromancer* without giving me the chance to crack a smile.)

Finally, there's "Night of the Living Oldpharts," a story

during which you have my permission to smile if you wish. You can tell from the title that it's vaguely inspired by a certain movie that's a favorite of people who love camp and other forms of horror. Once again I'm treating fandom as a microcosm of a world — but this time of a fantasy world, which somehow seems more appropriate anyway.

There you have it, a sampler of pieces I've written as a fan and as a professional. They're different each from each, but should you wish to get analytical you'll be able to find themes, thoughts, touches of style and pacing that rattle and echo throughout, between...

Two worlds? No, there's only one — because each is a microcosm of the other, each the heart of its counterpart. (Say now, there's an idea for a science fiction story. I hope Bob Shaw hasn't already written it.)

— Terry Carr

# CONTENTS

# ACKNOWLEDGMENTS

I would to like thank the following people for all the help they've provided in producing this book. Our typists were Claire Anderson, Dave Anderson, Jill Eastlake, Pam Fremon, Rick Katze, Laurie Mann, Mark Olson, Priscilla Pollner, Mark Trumpler, Pat Vandenberg, and Lee Winter. The production and typesetting crew were Sharon Sbarsky, Greg Thokar, Pam, Rick, Priscilla, and Mark Trumpler. George Flynn and Sue Hammond were our Master Proofers and copy editors. As usual Rick Katze handled all of the contract arrangements. And finally I would like to express my greatest thanks to Jim Mann, who has been Senior Supervising Editor for the duration of the production of this book. Jim has been patient enough to teach me how to do all of this so that he can retire along with the rest of NESFA's previous editors. Thanks to you all.

Andy Cowan, Editor
Marlboro, MA
June 1986

# BETWEEN
# TWO
# WORLDS

# THE CHASER

Alan Austen, hopeful as a new faned reading his first review, went up certain dark and creaky stairs in a dimly lit neighborhood, and peered at the names on each door on the dimly lit landing before he found the name he wanted.

He pushed open this door and entered, following instructions on a postcard he had received the day before. The postcard had said, "This is a test. Bring this card to the address below and examine my stock of extraordinary fan supplies. Everlasting typewriter ribbons, psi beanies, hoax-finders, enchanted duplicators, oil-of-midnight candles, foolproof hektoes, potions of all kinds. Featured this week: the fan-success pill. (All merchandise guaranteed. No sticky machines.)"

Inside the door, an old man sat quietly reading a book called *The Necronomicon*. Behind him were many shelves filled with bottles, cans, and packages. A door to the left led into a room in which the only light seemed to come, dimly, from half-seen machines of all sizes and shapes.

"Sit down, Mr. Austen," said the old man. Alan sat down.

"I am interested," said Alan, "in your fan-success pill.

That seems to be — er — quite extraordinary, as your ad said."

"My dear young fan," replied the old man, "my stock in trade is limited — I don't deal in used magazines or rubber stamps — but such as it is, it is varied. Nothing I sell has effects which could be described as precisely ordinary."

"The fact is —" began Alan.

"Here, for example," interrupted the old man, reaching for a bottle from the shelf, "is a liquid which is quite palatable, like blog almost, but which induces the purest form of gafia."

"Do you mean people take potions in order to quit fandom?" cried Alan.

"Some do," said the old man. "Others find gafia quite easy — a natural talent, if you will. For those for whom it comes hard, there is the potion. A way of extricating oneself from too many unimportant responsibilities and imagined obligations. A way to get out of the rut. 'Fandom is just a goddam habit.' A gafia potion, yes."

"I want nothing of that sort," said Alan.

"Just as well, no doubt," said the old man. "The price for one teaspoonful — sufficient for all but the most hardened fan — is five thousand dollars. Never a penny less."

"I hope you have less expensive mixtures," said Alan.

"Oh, my, yes," said the old man. "It would be foolish to charge that sort of price for the fan-success pill, for example. Neofans who need them never have five thousand dollars — else they wouldn't need the pill. Eh? They'd pay the top fan-writers to write for their fanzines and so forth. Right?"

"Oh, of course," said Alan.

"I look at it this way," said the old man. "Please a patron with one article, and he will come back when he needs another. Even if it *is* more costly. You see? He will save up for it, if necessary."

"So," said Alan, "you really do have pills that will ensure fannish success. And they are not just — just — er . . ."

"Oh, no," said the old man. "Their effects are permanent. This is no fly-by-night establishment. Within two years, your fan-writing will be collected together in one volume. *The Incompleat Austen,* perhaps. Or *The Alan Austen Reader."*

"Dear me!" said Alan. "How very enticing!"

"A permanent evidence of your mark on fandom," said the old man. "Your works collected. If you wish, a new collection issued every year thereafter. Volume Two, Volume Three, like that. An annual affair."

"I can hardly believe it," said Alan. "My stories have been rejected by every fan editor I know of."

"They will no longer reject them," said the old man. "Instead, they will write you letters by the score, asking for your stories. They will want you to write columns for them, articles, poetry, your autobiography!"

"Oh, my!"

"Never a day will go by without at least one request for you to write something. You will spend all your free time writing for your public. That is," he said, "all of it except that spent publishing your own fanzine."

"My own fanzine!" breathed Alan.

"Your own fanzine. The number one fanzine, of course. The focal-point fanzine. Contributions by all the other top writers in fandom — the others besides yourself, of course. A long letter column in each issue — fifteen, twenty pages. Each issue will make up seventy-five pages of the best of all possible material."

"Seventy-five pages!" said Alan. "That *is* a lot!"

"Yes, it's a lot," said the old man. "But as a contribution to fandom it will be worth the long hours required for its stenciling, of course."

"Oh, of course!"

"Through all your most tiring days," said the old man, "that thought will be there to comfort you. You will be doing a service for fandom. A hollow comfort?"

"Oh, no!" said Alan. "It will fulfill me!"

"No young fan could have phrased it better," smiled the old man. "I think you will make a fine Number One Fan, Mr. Austen."

"That's odd," said Alan. "You know my name. How is that? You must have sent out many postcards."

"Just one," said the old man. "I sent only one postcard, and that to you."

"But why is that?" asked Alan.

"I have only one fan-success pill for sale at the moment," said the old man. "Naturally, *everyone* can't be Number One Fan — the field is limited by definition. I sent only one card. I won't have another pill for sale for some time. A year, perhaps two years."

Alan was lost for a moment in daydreams. "Number One Fan," he murmured. "How much do you charge for this wonderful pill?"

"It is not so dear," said the old man, "as the gafia potion. No. That is five thousand dollars. One has to be older than you are, and tired, to indulge in that sort of thing. One has to save up for it."

"But the pill?" asked Alan.

"Oh, that," said the old man, handing him a small bottle containing a black pill enveloped in cotton. "That is just a dollar."

"I can't tell you how grateful I am," said Alan, paying him.

"I like to oblige," said the old man. "Then patrons come back, later, and want more expensive things. Here you are."

"Thank you again," said Alan. "Goodbye."

"*Au revoir,*" said the old man.

# A COMPLETE MYSTERY

"I can't make any sense out of this ruddy case!" grumbled Inspector Lockridge as he sank back into the deep cushions of the divan. The Inspector furrowed his shiny forehead over dark eyebrows and stared moodily into his teacup. He was obviously not a happy man at this particular moment.

Sitting directly across the room from him was a man little more than half his height, it seemed, though that could not have been the case: Inspector Lockridge was well over six feet tall, thin and ascetic-looking in his early forties, but the man whom he faced must have been no more than a foot shorter than him by any tape measure. It was his breadth of figure that made the contrast so striking... that, and the precisely short cravat which he wore peeping out from beneath his dark vest. The smaller man must have out-weighed the Inspector by a stone, but he carried his weight easily. It was his manner: his step was brisk, the movements of his pudgy but expressive hands free and easy, his eyes twinkling with a humor all their own. The wart on the side of his left nostril seemed particularly good-humored.

This man was Honore Goriot, a man so familiar and respected in law enforcement circles that he was known as Papa Goriot to most of the police forces of the continent. The underworld called him by another name, but their respect for him was no less sharp. Goriot was the mild-mannered scourge of the lawless, the quiet-spoken detective who had brought about the downfall of more criminals than any police officer alive. And yet Goriot worked alone, calling upon the established agencies only occasionally for research into fingerprint evidence or a matter of the *modus operandi* of a criminal at large.

He sat quietly in the hard-backed chair, his wide Gallic mouth (he was actually Belgian) drawn almost imperceptibly back into a half-smile, his fingers toying idly with the cup beside him.

"Perhaps, *mon ami,* you do yourself an injustice," he said. "A few clues, and the use of the little gray cells..." He tapped the side of his head.

Inspector Lockridge raised his eyes quickly to meet those of Goriot; he stared hard at the smaller man for a moment before dropping his gaze tiredly. "Oh, there are clues," he said. "But what good are clues which do not fit together, which form no pattern?"

The light in Goriot's eye had never been more pronounced than it was now. "There are times," he said softly, "when such evidence is of the best. *Enfin,* we shall see."

Again the Inspector raised his gaze to meet that of the small detective, but this time he held that meeting. "What do you mean?" he asked. His words came slowly, but there was a gathering sharpness about them nonetheless.

Goriot shrugged. "No murder case is unsolvable. One commits such an action and hopes to leave no effect other than the death which was its object, *n'est-ce pas?* But there

are always ramifications of every action we make. *Bien...
c'est ça.* It is time to call the household together, Inspector."

The tall man winced slightly at these words. One could
almost see his self-respect crumbling under the quiet barrage
of Goriot's certainty. "You intend to confront them with a
solution?" he asked.

*"Bien sur,"* Goriot said simply.

Inspector Lockridge sat unmoving for several long mo-
ments. As a case-hardened veteran of many dealings with
criminals he had learned well to veil the movements of
his thoughts, but Goriot could see at least eight different
emotions flicker in succession behind his eyes.

"Mrs. Parkinson was my aunt," the Inspector said slowly.
"She was murdered in cold blood, for no apparent reason...
a monstrous crime. I had hoped that *I...* " He cleared the
shadows from his furrowed forehead with a determined
effort. "But no matter. Justice will be done, in any case." He
rose and left the room.

Goriot watched him leave and then, one eyebrow lifted
almost imperceptibly, rose and walked quickly to the
writing-desk at one side of the room. The drawers and
compartments of the desk were all locked, as they had been
when the victim had been found lying bloody beside it. The
top of the desk was bare, save for a single scrap of paper on
which was written: "Cabbage." An inky line trailed jaggedly
across the page from there, presumably made when the lady
had been struck down from behind. The pen lay in the corner
of the desk, the ink coagulated upon it. Goriot wrinkled his
stubby nose in distaste: no one had wiped the pen after its
use.

*"La plume de ma tante est sur la table,"* murmured Goriot,
and turned as the members of the family and the servants
began to arrive.

Smithers, the gardener, was the first to enter. He was a dark man, heavily built; his hands were large, with heavy knuckles. But his fingernails were clean, Goriot noted. The man hesitated inside the doorway, then took the seat in the corner to which Goriot waved him.

Miss Jane Parkinson seemed agitated when she arrived. She was the murdered woman's daughter, and her eyes were red-rimmed from weeping. She was petite, with dark hair caught in a bun at the nape of her neck; she immediately sat on the divan and drew her feet beneath her. Her gaze rested on the floor. Goriot remembered that not once in the past three days had the woman met his eyes for more than a flickering second.

Bertha, the cook and housekeeper, stepped heavily through the door and took a position standing by the wall. There was a sullen defiance in her eyes, as though she resented the very implication that she might have anything to do with the murder. Such a disposition, thought Goriot, could lead a woman to *le crime passionel.*

Herbert Parkinson, the husband of the deceased, came slowly into the room and sank into a chair as though he had strength for no more movement in this life. He raised his eyes curiously to meet Goriot's, but his gaze too faltered before the calm eyes of the little detective and he stared idly, almost vacantly, at his right hand. Goriot had known Parkinson for over a year; through him he had taken an interest in this case. He knew that Parkinson was left-handed. *Eh bien.*

The last member of the household was the maid, Sally Bray. She tossed herself next to Miss Jane on the divan, fussing with her skirts for some seconds. She was full of life, this one, thought Goriot, and smiled. A charming creature . . . but he had noticed that her light chatter often served the purpose of evading more personal matters. Was she merely light-headed? Or, *enfin,* was any young woman as senseless as she seemed?

Inspector Lockridge followed the others into the room and seated himself in the hard-backed chair which Goriot had vacated. He shook a cigarette from its case and thrust it between his thin lips. "All right, Goriot, let's have a go," he said, and struck a match.

Goriot nodded his head brusquely. *"Bien.* We shall begin by indulging in personalities, if you will excuse my vulgarity. For crime, and murder *en particulière,* is always a matter of personality. It is not merely a matter of clues."

He paced lightly back and forth before them, his shoes pressing soundlessly into the deep rug. He stopped at the edge of the bloodstain by the writing-desk and gazed pensively down at it.

"All that we have of your aunt in this room is a dried bloodstain, is it true, Lockridge?"

The Inspector frowned, almost in anger. "That does seem a bit crude, Goriot. We can all see it; you needn't call it to our attention. Yes, that's all we have of her here, and it's a beastly reminder, I must say."

Goriot smiled apologetically. "Forgive me, *mon collègue —* I wish merely to make a point. For *the bloodstain is not all that we have of Mrs. Parkinson.* We have more, much more."

Inspector Lockridge sat forward in his seat. Miss Jane uttered a little gasp, and Bertha grunted with ill-tempered disdain. The others remained impassive.

"We have her very personality with us today," Goriot continued. "That is the heart of the matter — everyone in this room knew Mrs. Parkinson, and everyone here felt toward her in a certain way. And that, Inspector, is the very best sort of clue."

"Get along with it," the police officer grumbled.

*"Mon plaisir,"* Goriot murmured, and gave a little bow. He turned to Miss Jane and regarded her politely. "Let us consider *your* relationship with Mrs. Parkinson. Perhaps there was some...friction? *Hein?"*

Miss Jane paled visibly. Her voice came tremulously: "But there was never...I mean..."

"Is it not true, *ma petite,* that on the morning of the fatality you had quarreled with your mother? Something about a silk parasol you wished to purchase? Mrs. Parkinson was, I understand, a frugal woman."

Miss Jane's eyes flashed suddenly, and she met Goriot's gaze defiantly. "She was a miser, my mother! All my life I had to beg her for money for the littlest things!"

"And you are a woman of thirty," murmured Goriot. "Yes, it must have been frustrating."

"I am twenty-nine until next month," said Miss Jane, again withdrawing into herself.

"Well, no matter," Goriot shrugged. "I point out merely that there was friction between you...*n'est-ce pas?* And during a heated moment, harsh words, anger overcomes you...*alors,* you have struck her down with a copy of the *New International Unabridged Dictionary!"*

"No!" protested the young woman. She raised tear-brimmed eyes for a moment. "That dictionary has never been used in this house since we bought it. I...I always went to *McCann's Home Dictionary.* There it is, on the table...you may see for yourself."

Goriot fingered the slim volume which she indicated.

"You are correct...the edges of these pages bear evidence of frequent use, which the murder weapon lacked. *Bien*...let us pass on." He turned to Smithers, the gardener. "There is some talk that you have had...how shall I say...*une liaison* with a woman, *monsieur. Une liaison dangereuse,* perhaps?"

Smithers' bulky body gave a start: his head jerked up. "Where did you hear that?"

"Ah, there are *toujours* the gossips. It is said...forgive me, Herbert, *mon ancien*"—he glanced at Mr. Parkinson—"...that your gardener had been seeing Mrs. Parkinson."

Smithers' face reddened. "That isn't true," he said in a low voice. "I had been seeing someone else, and we knew there would be talk, so we...deflected the gossip onto her. People will believe such a romance more readily these days, and there is less chance of anyone speaking of it to the master."

Goriot raised his eyebrows halfway to his thinly cropped gray hair. "That explains much, *monsieur*. Both of you wished to avoid dismissal—quite understandable. And the young lady..." He turned to Sally Bray, the maid. "The young lady is now full of life, we may say, so the secret must come out in any event. Ah, but this is interesting! Had Mrs. Parkinson, perhaps, discovered your secret and threatened to reveal it to her husband?"

*"That's not so!"* exclaimed the young woman. Her face fell. "She...she had known of it for some time, but she had never said anything about speaking to Mr. Parkinson."

"Ah, but perhaps she had heard of the gossip which concerned her, and had become angered? And then you, or *Monsieur* Smithers, had found it necessary to...?"

"I won't have this!" shouted Smithers. "You're playing with us, Mr. Goriot, and unnecessarily, too! You know we had nothing to do with it!"

*"C'est ça,"* murmured Goriot. "You were together in the greenhouse at the time...as one of the boys of the neighborhood who was watching you with *la fascination* has testified."

Sally Bray's face reddened and she tore at the handkerchief in her hands.

Goriot turned to Bertha. "And what are we to say of you, *mademoiselle?* What were your relations with Mrs. Parkinson?"

Bertha drew herself up angrily. "I never had *any* relations with Mrs. Parkinson."

"Because she is not your type," said Sally Bray sweetly, and then suddenly reddened again and turned her attention back to her handkerchief. Bertha glared at her, tight-lipped.

Inspector Lockridge sat forward impatiently. "Look here, Goriot, is all this quite necessary? Damn it, man, we've gathered the entire household here for you...now if you have anything to say, then say it!"

Goriot sighed quietly. "It is necessary in each case to be thorough, but perhaps we have reached the moment for *la vérité.*" He paused, rubbing his index finger idly along the side of his nose.

"Let us consider the evidence, *mes amis.* The unfortunate woman was sitting at her writing-desk when the blow fell...she has written the single word 'Cabbage.' We assume from this that she was writing a shopping list. Ah, but are we correct in this?"

Goriot laid his hand on the heavy volume next to him. "The murder weapon is found by her side. One page is turned down: this page contains the words Okra to Ophthalmia. Is it a clue? The night before the fatal occurrence Mr. Parkinson has a brief dispute with his wife about various sorts of tea—Oolong is one of the words on this page. *Bien.* We have a connection. Mr. Parkinson...*mon ami,* have you not on the night in question taken down the unabridged dictionary?"

Herbert Parkinson stared at Goriot. "I looked up that word," he said levelly.

*"Très bien.* Herbert, I know you...you are not a

punctilious man. You forgot to put the book away. *N'est-ce pas?"*

Parkinson's face suddenly grew uneasy with guilt. After a moment, he whispered, "I forgot to put it away. My wife often lectured me about such lapses."

"It is a point of friction," Goriot said. "Another link. Now, the next morning shortly before noon Mrs. Parkinson is found dead at her writing-desk, struck down by this very dictionary. The corner of the volume is bent in from the blow." He gazed sharply around the room. An air of expectancy hung over everyone in it. "The book is damaged from the blow. I ask you, *mes amis,* is this the work of a punctilious person? Ah, no."

Herbert Parkinson was frowning.

"Now...as to the matter of the word Mrs. Parkinson has written. It has confused me for some time. Herbert, I know that you love cabbage. Should I assume, then, that you would strike down your wife because she has ordered cabbage for your meal? Ah, *non. Ce n'est pas raisonnable."*

Parkinson relaxed a bit, and sat back in his chair.

*"But,"* said Goriot, and that single syllable brought them all to attention once again. "We are overlooking a possibility. Perhaps Mrs. Parkinson wrote this word *after* the blow was struck. *Eh bien,* it is an accusation." Goriot stepped lightly to the writing-desk and picked up the piece of paper. "'Cabbage,'" he said. *"J'accuse!"*

There was bewilderment on everyone's face. Goriot smiled.

"Herbert, I know you. I knew your wife. *Mon ami,* I have been a guest in your home many times, and I have ears, *c'est vrai?* I have heard your wife when she calls you by her pet name. She calls you 'my cabbage.' *Non?"*

Herbert Parkinson was startled. His face took on a sudden

pallor, and perspiration formed on his forehead.

Inspector Lockridge stood up. "Parkinson, you were never welcome in our family!" he spat. "I remember the words of my mother — *your dead wife's sister.* 'A rum bod,' she said. God knows how many times she said that of you!"

Goriot regarded his friend and sighed. "I am sorry, *mon ami,*" he said.

Parkinson looked wildly around the room. "This is madness," he said. "You are jesting again, Goriot!"

Goriot's voice was soft when he said, "I do not jest at the end, *monsieur.*"

"But you're wrong!" Parkinson said shrilly. "Wrong!"

"Am I?" murmured Goriot.

"Goriot... please. You were with me that morning... we were in the parlor. We played chess for an hour or more, and I never once left the room! Goriot, you must remember!"

Goriot's face clouded. *"Nom d'un nom,"* he whispered.

"The parlor is at the other end of the house!" Parkinson said. *"In the other wing.* I couldn't have done this thing!"

Goriot's round face had a look of horror. The wart on the side of his nose quivered. "You are right, *mon ami,* I have made the mistake!"

He paced the length of the room twice, his steps heavy. Everyone's eyes were upon him. He faced them bleakly, and raised his shoulders in an elaborate Gallic shrug. (He was actually Belgian.) "He is innocent, Inspector." Goriot shook his head sadly, and walked slowly to the door.

The assembled servants and relatives watched him, stunned. "Then who did it?" Inspector Lockridge said in exasperation. "Damn it, man! Who is the guilty one?"

Goriot paused in the doorway and surveyed the faces which were turned to him. He frowned, and pursed his lips. "Ach, it is a problem," he admitted. Then he threw up his hands and left the room, shaking his head. They heard his voice in the hall saying, *"C'est un mystère complet."* And the outer door shut behind him.

In the silence which followed, Herbert Parkinson said, "It's no wonder, him forgetting about the game. He lost. Mate in ten plays, too."

*With apologies to and admiration for Agatha Christie*
*— T.C.*

# THE CONVENTION THAT
## COULDN'T BE KILLED

Well, maybe Worldcons *won't* just keep on getting bigger and bigger. SunCon in Miami Beach drew just over 2,000 attendees, almost a thousand fewer than last year's Worldcon. It was still fairly crowded and hectic, but less so than Worldcons have been for many years (Aussiecon excepted). Besides, the Fontainebleau Hotel was a huge, sprawling site where you could spend ten minutes walking from one meeting room to another even if you didn't stop off in the bar; there was plenty of room in which people could move around.

"Huge" may not be the *mot juste* for the Fontainebleau; maybe "gross" would describe it better. It's the premier Garish Hotel from Miami Beach's days of affluence and its decor reflects the tastes of the *nouveaux riches* who traditionally made up its clientele. Marble pillars are common, and the main lobby features enormous glistening chandeliers the size of tugboats. "The style of this hotel is High Tacky," I said.

The smaller number of attendees was attributed largely to poor public relations on the part of the Convention

Committee — who, even more than usual, came in for a lot of criticism. The del Reys and Wollheims stayed away because of conflicts with the Committee, or so went the rumors; andy offutt, President of SFWA, stayed away for the same reason. People said the Committee had been "fascistic"; people said the con was badly organized because the Committee members didn't live anywhere near Miami Beach; people complained about a lot of things to do with the Committee. No doubt the Committee made some goofs, but as I was moved to say several times during the convention, "No Committee can ruin a Worldcon, and this one is proving it."

A Committee may choose a lousy hotel, may antagonize some people into staying away, may make unwise programming decisions, but what does it matter? Two thousand fans, readers, writers, artists, editors, and publishers gather under one roof for a weekend of hijinx and business, and how can anyone stop them from having a good time? Put me in a room with Sid Coleman, Dave Hartwell, Lizzy Lynn, Howard Waldrop, Gardner Dozois, Ginjer Buchanan, Sherry Gottlieb, Ed Bryant, Ted White, Jack Dann, Marta Randall, Lee Hoffman, Tom Perry, Avedon Carol, Bob Silverberg, Jay Kay Klein, George R. R. Martin, Lesleigh Luttrell, and all the rest of that crowd, and I'm going to have a good time.

It didn't start out all that well. I flew to Miami Beach with Bob Silverberg, Marta Randall, and Lizzy Lynn, and the in-flight movie was *Smokey and the Bandit,* which features Burt Reynolds in one car chase after another. Bob and I serconly read science fiction rather than watch the movie, but Marta and Lizzy happily donned headphones and chortled their way through. Bob was reading my *Best SF of the Year #5,* which struck me as ironic since I was reading 1977 sf magazines, researching *Best SF #7.* Sometime during the flight Bob turned to me and said, "I just read 'Retrograde Summer'—*now* I know why everyone's talking about John Varley." Marta laughed aloud, lifted off an earphone, and said, "Did you see what he did to that truck?"

We landed in Miami and Bob picked up the Hertz Pinto he'd reserved. There were ants in the car; as we drove out to the causeway leading to Miami Beach, Bob said, "It's a tropical climate, that's why. Look at all the greenery." Indeed, Florida seemed astonishingly green to us after two years of drought in California; besides, there was something falling from the sky, something...well, wet. Rain? I could hardly believe it, but rain it was, and lots of it, a torrent.

Somewhere out on the causeway, pelted by rain and lashed by crosswinds, we noticed that the car was acting funny— bumpy ride, and getting bumpier. "Rough road," said Bob. "Flat tire," said Lizzy, so we stopped and Marta got out and checked all the tires. "Nothing," she said, so we proceeded another half mile while the ride got rougher. Finally Bob pulled over again, and this time when Marta looked at the tires she came back saying, "Jee-*zus!* We don't have any tire at all in the right rear!" We all got out in the pelting rain and looked: the steel-belted radial had completely shredded, leaving only a wheel-rim surrounded by mangled rubber and wires that looked like Shredded Wheat. Marta went to a nearby call-box to tell Hertz to get another car here soon, while I stared bemusedly at the remains of the tire and muttered, "I *thought* something was wrong when the ants deserted the car."

The rain stopped, and we got out and stood by the car for forty-five minutes waiting for a Hertzperson, examining the roadside rocks for fossils (found one), occasionally seeing fan-types pass by in taxis on the way to the Fontainebleau. Sherry Gottlieb and Larry Niven waved to us from a taxi.

Five cars stopped and their drivers asked if we needed help; I was impressed by Southern Friendliness till I noticed that at least two of the cars had out-of-state plates. (Besides, Miami Beach is the Sixth Borough of New York City.) Eventually our replacement car arrived and we proceeded to the hotel without further incident.

We all checked in, I met Lizzy for a quick dinner in the coffee shop, and then we went off to look for the action. What we found was an elevator that took us to B, and K, and P, but not the fifth floor. "I feel like a character in a Kafka novel," said L. We gave up and went to a Meet the Authors party. (There was one Thursday night and another Friday night; I forget why, and maybe the Committee does too.) Oh, and I stopped to register for the con — it took exactly two minutes and eight seconds, which was a bit of an improvement over the forty-five minutes it had taken at Kansas City last year, so evidently this Committee did something right.

Among the Authors I met was...Lee Hoffman! Whee! Hadn't seen her in six years. We hugged and danced around manically for a while, then I asked her what she'd been doing lately: "You're a Big Name Western Writer now, aren't you? Won a Spur Award and all that." "Yeeaahh...but there's no money in westerns. I'm writing a historical now." "Why not write more science fiction? — there's lots of money in sf right now." "Well, maybe...but you know I was always a fakefan."

Ted White was there. "I have a new career," he told me. "I'm a radio deejay now; I have a regular program where I play all the progressive rock I want. I did one program, right after Elvis Presley died, where I announced a Tribute to Elvis Presley and then played three of his most famous numbers, only recorded by better people. Then I said, 'That concludes our Tribute to Elvis Presley.'" I remarked, "Wow, you must've gotten plenty of calls complaining about *that,*" and Ted's face lit up in a grin. "No, actually we didn't get a single one. Nobody who listens to this program knows me as Bitching Ole Ted White. It's terrific!" "Don't worry, they'll learn," I assured him.

Later I went up to the Berkley-Putnam suite, where Dave Hartwell was hosting the standard drunken party of the sort at which the next two years of science fiction are negotiated late at night over vodka-and-root-beer highballs. I talked with Larry Niven, who told me that despite his many laurels he's being twitted by Jerry Pournelle because Larry never won the John W. Campbell Award for Best New Writer (the award hadn't yet existed when Larry had started writing): "And I can't do anything about it, because I'm no longer eligible!" I thought about that a moment, and my fannish instincts came back to me in a rush: "Why don't you take a penname," I said, "and write all your best stuff under that name?" He shook his head. "Wouldn't be fair to the *real* new writers," he said. "Well then, just wait till you're nominated and the votes are counted but the awards haven't been engraved, then call the Committee and withdraw so the second-place writer can get the award." Larry shuffled his feet and thought about this. "There's one problem," he said. "What if I don't win?" "... Um," I said. We discussed various alternative methods for a while but came up with nothing workable. Finally Larry said, "Let's talk about this some more tomorrow when I'm sober." "Nah," I said. "When we're sober we won't be interested in talking about this. Let's continue this discussion at the next drunken party." He said okay, but we never got back to the subject despite many drunken parties thereafter, so I'm still not sure how Larry Niven is going to meet the challenge of Jerry Pournelle.

It was, as you may have gathered, late at night. A number of people began filtering out of the main room of the Berkley-Putnam suite into the bedroom searching for breathable air and a place to sit down. Among them were Marta Randall, Jack Dann, and Sherry Gottlieb, who invented a game which I encountered when I entered the room. "Anybody who steps across the threshold," said Jack, "has to tell us when they first Did It, and how old they were, and where." He thought a moment, then added, "And don't tell us you don't remember, because *everybody* remembers." So for the next hour, as the party in the main room kept getting more and more crowded and the number of people in our room grew to a dozen or more, we were regaled with funny stories from one entrant after another. No names were used, of course, nor were there any salacious details; it was just that one's First Time *always* seems to have its ludicrous aspects...fumbling, bad planning, wondering what-do-I-do-now, etc. We were all struck by awe and glee when one person said matter-of-factly, "It was two o'clock in the afternoon, in a cemetery."

One young woman upon being queried hesitated, then asked, "You mean with a man or a woman?" Jack waved a hand airily: "Doesn't matter. Whichever was first." "Goats and chickens count too," I said helpfully.... It was a very Silly party, not at all the sort of thing neofans probably imagine goes on at gatherings of distinguished pros, but as I've said often over the years, pros are sillier than fans anytime.

Sometime during this party, one of the convention's important lacks was corrected: Sid Coleman arrived, just off a plane from Istanbul or Crete or somewhere. He was suffering from jet lag and unable to join in the general hilarity very much, but when Jack said, "I'm getting tired of this First Time game; let's start asking about everyone's most embarrassing moment," Sid responded: "That's the same question!"

The next day I moderated a "Women in Science Fiction" panel on which I appeared with Phyllis Eisenstein, Marta Randall, and Lizzy Lynn. I was the moderator because I arrived last and everyone else had already said a firm "No!" But I like moderating panels, and this one went well; I enjoyed it. A fairly typical presentation on the subject, but some new things were said and the familiar things were said well. (Ray Nelson, when I was talking to him some weeks after the con, told me he's tired of the "Women in SF" panels and wishes they, the panels, would go away; I predicted they'll be a staple item in the programming of every Worldcon for at least five more years, because more and more women are beginning to read sf and they're interested in them, which means these panels will continue to draw good-sized audiences.) This one had about sixty people in the room, which was an unusually large turnout for the program at SunCon. Most presentations had far fewer people: I saw, for instance, a dialogue between Fred Pohl, a big name, and Jack Williamson, who was Guest of Honor fergodsake, and there were only forty people listening.

I was on a couple of other panels, too. The first was "The Bay Area: Science Fiction's Left Bank," on which Marta, Lizzy, Bob Silverberg, and I described the workings of a social scene in which nearly half the people are sf writers. My favorite anecdote was about the time Marta, who lives three houses down the street from Carol and me, submitted a chapter from a forthcoming novel as a short story for *Universe*. I didn't think the chapter stood well by itself, so the next day I phoned her at home, figuring she'd be at her office and I could make history by becoming the first editor ever to reject a story to an answering machine. She was home that day, though, so I may never get that slot in the Guinness Book of Sci Fi Records. That evening I walked down to Marta's to return the manuscript, and complained that she hadn't enclosed return postage. (More recently Marta submitted a short story which I liked, but I goofed and called her at the office to tell her I wanted to buy it, thus losing my chance to become the first editor to *accept* a story from an answering machine.)

Monday afternoon Ted White and I did a "dialogue" panel on "Fandom in the Sixties," held in the small fan-programming room that someone had hidden off in a corner somewhere, reachable only through a series of secret passages. (Hm, maybe *that* was where the Kafka elevator went!) We'd discussed earlier how we should handle this, and agreed that I'd tell about everything wonderful Ted had done in fandom in the sixties, and he'd talk about all the wonderful stuff I'd done. It didn't quite work out that way (well, we weren't *really* serious, you understand). Ted showed up that day very hyper, and he talked a blue streak...the "dialogue" nearly turned into a monologue, and if Ted hadn't been saying such interesting things — not all about me, either — I'd have killed him. We talked about sixties fandom for our scheduled hour, then were told that the "Fandom in the Fifties" panel, which had been scheduled right after ours, had been canceled because Bob Silverberg had elected to go look at botanical gardens instead of talking about Seventh Fandom, Warren A. Frieberg, and Peter J. Vorzimer. So we called up Lee Hoffman from the audience — she'd been scheduled on the fifties panel — and continued for another hour.

A strange and moderately wonderful thing happened when we started talking about fannish fanzines and sercon fanzines: Ted was rhapsodizing over *Hyphen* when Ed Wood boomed from the audience, "I WAS ON THE *HYPHEN* MAILING LIST AND I USED TO DROP EVERY COPY INTO THE WASTEBASKET WITHOUT EVEN OPEN-ING IT!" Ted told him he was crazy and had no taste and they promptly got into a loud argument while I sat there thinking to myself that this was exactly the sort of thing that used to happen in fandom in the fifties and all the newer fans in the audience were seeing history come alive. I finally diverted the argument onto some safe topic, like maybe *Sky Hook,* but I kept expecting to see Harlan Ellison come striding into the room announcing, "I've got Dean A. Grennell quotecards, and you can't beat 'em, buddy!"

There were lots and lots of parties at the con, and I found myself hanging out alternately with the feminists and the pros. (Sometimes they were the same.) I went to the Women's Apa party, courtesy of Jennifer Bankier and Avedon Carol, but left after a while when I noticed there were more men than women there. I wandered into the Pocket Books party, the Ace party, the Berkley-Putnam party... You know, in the past there's usually been just one publisher's party per night at conventions, but sf has become so profitable these days that the publishers and editors turned out in droves to try to lure authors into their clutches. It wasn't a cutthroat business, though: at the end of the Pocket Books party, Adele Hull sent all the leftover liquor up to the Berkley-Putnam party, for instance.

That Pocket Books party was a lot of fun, by the way. It was held in a fairly large room off the lobby with the pros gathered round various bar-type tables to chat and carouse. I spent most of my time at what I called the Silly Table, where Howard Waldrop, Gardner Dozois, Dave Hartwell, and a bunch of other zanies held forth; next to us was the

Hard Science table, where Poul Anderson, Hal Clement, and others discussed less important things. I remember Gardner telling us about the Conan the Barbarian Pizza Parlor, which actually exists somewhere in Texas; we all immediately began to make up a variety of fast-food establishments like Fafhrd's Felafel and The Big Brak. And I remember the wonderful t-shirt Howard Waldrop was wearing: it showed two gaunt hands reaching up from the beltline to clutch frantically at his chest. "What does it mean?" Dave Hartwell asked. "I don't know," Howard said. "It's a good writer trying to get out," I explained, and Howard fell off his chair.

The fan programming in that little room off a broom closet included a couple of feminist panels, too: "Sexism in Fandom," etc. The panelists were sometimes quite explicit in warning new female fans about which pros were Grabbers, etc.; it was refreshing to hear truth instead of mythology over the mike at a convention. Nor was it as humorless as feminists are imagined to be. During one panel Ann Weiser said to the men in the audience, "Hey, we don't want to be called girls, or chicks, or broads, or ladies, or any of those. Call us..." "Dykes," said Avedon Carol. "Right! Dykes!" Ann cried, raising a clenched fist and then collapsing under the table in laughter.

I got to meet all sorts of people I'd been wanting to meet, like Jim Baen and Kirby McCauley and Jim Frenkel (who did a wonderful boggle when, after we'd been joking together at the Silly Table for ten minutes, he glanced at my name tag and said, "You're *Terry Carr?* Wow!"). (Didn't stop him from rejecting a book proposal of mine, though.) Ran into Buz Wyeth of Harper's in the huckster room when I had just ten minutes to eat lunch and get to a panel I was on, so I didn't get to say much more than hello and see you again, which I didn't—a pity, because Buz is one of the nicest people in publishing. Sat next to Leigh Brackett at the Hugo banquet — I'm madly in love with her, but that's nothing new; I fell in love with her when I first read a story by her at age twelve. Carolyn Cherryh was at our table, also, and brought back from the podium both the John W. Campbell Award for Best New Writer and the Gandalf Award, which she accepted for Andre Norton. I talked with R. A. Lafferty during the Meet the Authors party; he said he's pretty much abandoned writing novels and is concentrating instead on short stories: "I'm like an aging relief pitcher — I can still throw smoke sometimes but mostly I get by on junk pitches."

Ed Bryant was a late arrival at the con. We'd heard he wouldn't be able to make it because he was laid up with the flu, but the second night as Sherry Gottlieb and I were heading for the SFWA suite we found him registering, suitcase at his feet. Sherry and I jumped all over him and hugged him and so on (Sherry hugged him a little more than I did), and he said, "You both now have forty-eight hours before you collapse from Venusian Slime Mold. Where's the action?" So we took him up to the SFWA suite and he walked in carrying his suitcase and a temperature of 102°. He seemed to have a good time, though. (Marta jumped all over him and hugged him, which possibly didn't hurt too much.)

One night I discussed with Art Saha, who works with Don Wollheim on *World's Best SF*, our methods of choosing the best stories of the year; we agreed that sticking pins in the contents pages of *F&SF* was almost as reliable as examining Gardner Dozois's entrails. I got interviewed for a radio program on KPFA and then for Ginjer Buchanan's column in *Cosmos*. The last time I was interviewed for a science fiction magazine it was *Vertex*, which folded one issue later; I feel a little guilty about *Cosmos*.

I also ran into Gene Wolfe, with whom I'd had some correspondence over the fact that in *Best SF #6* I'd referred to him as "fiftyish." Since he's forty-five, he was shaken by this, and for several days I was getting a postcard-a-day pointing out that he was two years younger than Jacqueline Onassis, etc. On seeing him and exchanging greetings, I said gravely, "You're, uh, looking well, Gene," but he declined the gambit. He did, however, inform me that he was telling all his fellow writers that I was the best fortyish editor in the business, on Wednesdays.

There were lots and lots more parties. The Happy Gays Are Here Again party, hosted by Lizzy and Ctein, was a mob-scene both early and late, when I was there. The Hugo Losers' Party, hosted by Ace Books, was another highlight, though I deny the report that I took part in a "mock-orgy" there; actually I mostly stood on the sidelines and yelled "Cut that out!"

The Dead Dog Party in the SFWA suite was hilarious, though. All the zanies were there — zanies never sleep — and we amused ourselves listening to Gardner Dozois and George R. R. Martin recount the plot of some story a Clarion student had once turned in. (If it'd been half as good as their retelling it would have won a Hugo.) Various of the group at the party collaborated on an impromptu Conan satire which was given a dramatic reading by Jay Kay Klein and Bob Silverberg; we tried to convince Dave Hartwell to buy it, but he's too canny, even at 3:00 a.m. on the last night of a convention.

Sometime before dawn I went off to bed and giggled away what was left of the night. I kept thinking what a pity it was that the Convention Committee's most dastardly schemes had been so ineffectual all weekend, but I'd have bet that as the con came to its close the Committee members were somewhere giggling as incoherently as I was.

# VIRRA

*at the last
judgement we will all be trees*
— Margaret Atwood

I am walking; I am leaving my family, stepping past them day by day with hardly time for talk. Soon I shall be beyond them all, alone in fields where no roots touch.

I enter the dim clearing caused when Morden fell, bringing down with him three others of the family. Morden was one of our oldest, a giant who commanded the sun for thirty meters around. Lightning wounded him; years later he fell.

He is not dead. Fresh limbs reach straight up from his side while all others are crumbling and covered with ice; he has put all his blood into these new limbs. As I skirt his roots I see that two are still in place, still feeding. I trip over one, underground.

"Who is it?" asks Morden drowsily. "Who are you?"

"Wesk. I am Wesk." (I am dreadfully afraid of him. From earliest memory I have been told Morden would strangle the sun if I angered him.)

"Are you such a child, Wesk, that you are unable to feel when roots are near?" His voice is like winter blood, slow and thick.

"No, sir. I apologize for disturbing you. I was hurrying, and I am...afraid of you, sir."

Morden's laughter shakes his few leaves. "Then if you are not young, you lack understanding. How could one so old as I harm you? I lie on my side, catching the sun of noon, in shade the rest of the time. As the family grows over me, they take away even the noon."

I continue to move around him, feeling more carefully now as I slip my roots into the soil. Touching shallowly, barely penetrating the crisp ice that covers the ground even in summer.

"I am only passing," I say. "I shall not steal your sun."

"Where are you going? Is there more sun nearby?"

"No," I say, "but there was one who carried the sun with her. I am seeking her."

"Phaw! No one carries the sun; your roots are feeding in a cavern, your thoughts are starved."

I am nearly past Morden now, and I take courage. "But I saw her as she passed. She moved so quickly! She was small and unable to reach up for sun, but she carried light in her leaves. Her name is Virra."

Morden laughs deeply, causing my roots to tremble. I pause while I regrip the soil.

"So the quick ones still live," he says sardonically. "Beware of them, child; they are leftovers of the past. You might as well chase insects."

I move away from his root-drainage, but I hesitate and take time to feed in the soil. The sun is overhead now, and I stretch my branches upward; energy makes me giddy and foolish. "Insects exist only in tales for children," I say challengingly.

Morden shifts a limb with surprising swiftness in my direction; it intercepts the sun and I am left in shadow. "There *were* insects," he says. "I saw one during my second ring. The creature was hardly the size of a bud, but it flew faster than sight. Then it fell, and died. I believe it was the last."

"If you could not see it, how could you know of it?" I ask, edging away. There is another patch of sunlight nearby.

Again his root-shaking laughter comes, but I am farther away now and it hardly touches me. "I saw it when it had fallen. Later I ate it."

My curiosity is aroused. "What did it look like? Is it true that the insects had no leaves at all, no limbs?"

"It was ugly." The soil ripples around my roots: is Morden shuddering? "It searched my leaves for blossoms, and its touch was disgusting. We once reproduced by making leaves of pretty colors, you know, and scents like the whores of legend. We needed the insects then, to carry our seed, but no more."

He is rambling, as so many of the aged do. They love to talk of the past, and they seem to take special delight in grotesque tales. I drink the sun, and say respectfully, "How awful for you to be touched by such a thing."

"Yes, but the insect got nothing from me, or anyone. It fell, they all fell, and our pure seeds fed on the ground they enriched." Morden's voice is growing dimmer as the sun passes; he says dreamily, "The one of whom you speak is like the insects — fast-movers, strangers to peace. They will soon be gone."

I walk on, refusing to believe this. Virra was too beautiful for me to conceive of her dying. I remember the day she passed by me, moving so quickly she was almost gone before

I could hail her. Smaller than a sapling, she moved with sureness and grace, holding her supple, leaf-clustered limbs away from any touch with the rest of us.

"Wait," I called after her. "What are you?"

"I am Virra," she said. "And I can't wait; I'm returning to the field, where giants don't steal all the sun."

"We do not steal!" I cried; but she was nearly out of hearing range. She moved like limbs dancing in wind, her tiny roots touching the soil so shallowly that she seemed a mass of drifting leaves. But she was bright with inner-held sun. "Wait!" I called again. "I want to talk, to know you!"

"Then come to the field."

So I am walking, going on a journey longer than anyone in my family has made. I am still young; I can do it. Already I have passed Morden, who has grown silent in his shade.

The way is easy, for every year there are fewer of the family; there is always much room between us, and only the decaying bodies of fallen ancestors to block my path. I skirt them easily, for their roots have long since passed back into the earth. Mindless ferns offer no resistance to my passage.

I speak to no one for three days, moving quickly past the elders who stand dreaming in the sun, feeding in the earth below the ice. I pause for an hour here or there when I find unused sun. There is enough to replenish my energy, but my roots are becoming brittle and frayed from so much exposure to the air, and I notice I am leaving sap in my back-trail of rootings. Perhaps this journey will be more difficult than I thought.

I come to the place where Querca stands: she whose drainage extends for scores of meters from her trunk. Old as she is, she has recently dropped acorns; they punctuate my path, and several have melted through to the soil where they may take root. But I am fearful now because my own roots are bleeding. So I do not skirt her ground; I pause hardly an hour in sun before hurling myself across her shade.

I have traversed little more than half of it when she notices me. "Who is it?" she rumbles. "I can see you are young — have you no respect?"

Frightened, I blurt, "Have you seen one passing who carried sunlight in her leaves?"

I am able to take several more root-steps before I hear Querca chuckle (she drops an acorn that is still green), and she says, "You mean a *bush?*"

I shiver at the scorn in her voice and grip underground stones to steady myself. "I do not know her family, only that she lives in the field. What is a 'bush'?"

"Nothing; a bush is nothing. The ferns serve more purpose — at least they feed us when they die."

"But this . . . bush . . . has a mind. Her name is Virra."

Querca moves roots languidly, easing into soft, fresh earth. "Bushes have no memory. They have no need to remember, because they die so soon. What does it matter that this creature has a mind, if she cannot remember?"

Anxiety strikes me, and I pause in my traversal of Querca's icy shade. "Do you mean she will not remember me when I find her?"

"Hah! Remember you?" Querca slowly bends down over me, mingling her brittle branches with my young ones; I draw back involuntarily at the touch of dry, aging leaves. "The bushes have no past, nor any future. They have been driven from the family and must live alone in the open field. They sprout and die almost while we sleep."

"But she did *think!*" I am approaching the edge of Querca's shade now, and I take courage. "Even her thoughts were full of sunlight, and she did not hoard it as the old ones of the family do."

"Exactly," says Querca. "They throw away their thoughts and do not think them again." Her limbs lift away from mine as I pass from beneath her. "They waste the past just as they waste the sun. The sun is old; it was not always small as it is now. We have a duty to use its energy wisely, but *bushes* have no care for that."

"I shall ask her about wasting the sun," I say, moving at last out of Querca's shade and stepping carefully along a slope strewn with the crumbling remains of ancient ancestors. "But must we talk so much about the past?"

This rouses anger in Querca. *"Yes,* we must talk of it, for we used up the sun! We were so different — creatures that ran and ran, burning the sun within us till it was almost gone. The bushes are still like that: they are enemies!" She dips a giant bough. "How are you named?"

"I am Wesk. You do not know me."

"I shall know you in the future," Querca promises.

Her words are like frost, but I continue walking. I am free of Querca's shade and her voice now. I continue across the sun-dappled slope; the ancients of the family only glance at me. There are fewer of them than before, farther apart; I am coming to the family's edge, to the beginning of the field.

There is a strange form of life here, one that we see seldom in the deeper forest-family. Slim green trunks rise from the ground; they are only centimeters high, and they have no limbs. Their very trunks are their leaves. In that way they are like the ferns, but they are much simpler creatures. Ancient tales call them grasses, and this is as good a name as any, since, like the ferns, they cannot think and tell us a name for themselves.

Here too are the hermits, those who stand away from the edge of the family and think only to themselves. They spread great limbs wide and luxuriate in the energy of the red sun;

but their roots feed on the shallow loam of grasses, and it is said within the family that the hermits must one day return to our ground for sustenance.

My roots stumble across one of the hermits, for it lies shallow in the ground, and I wake her from a morning sleep. "Go away," she grumbles, still half dreaming. "Whoever you are."

I wonder briefly if she will ever be able to return to the family, since I have felt how stiff her roots are. "My name is Wesk. Have you seen the bush who recently visited the forest-family?"

"No. Go away from me." She spreads her limbs even more wide, hoping to induce me to move off in search of sun.

"Her name is Virra," I say, obediently hurrying toward the edge of the hermit's shade.

"I have nothing to do with bushes. I have nothing to do with anyone."

"Then farewell," I say as I reach the sun again, "and may your thoughts of yourself be rewarding." I intend this as an insult, for I am annoyed by the hermit's rejection, but as I move on I feel only contentment from her.

Night comes and goes before I reach the next hermit in my path; he stands alone on a small hillock held together by his roots, and so I surmise that he is old. I skirt his cold roots, which are surprisingly wide, and say, "I am seeking the bush named Virra; if you know where she is, tell me and I shall travel on more quickly."

I feel his roots move slowly as he rouses. "Virra?" he says sleepily. "Always Virra." He begins to lift his limbs to the morning sun. "Continue on your path and you will find Virra."

The blood surges within me and I press forward through the shallow grasses, giddy with the full sunlight of the field.

There are rocks and boulders here, many more than there are within the family; some thrust up out of the ground as though they could draw life from the sun. I come to a small creature, a being of leaves like Virra but no more than a summer old.

"I search for a bush who is named Virra," I say, hoping that this young creature will understand me.

"I am a bush," he says. "I am Virra."

"No. You are not the same Virra; you are too small, and you are male."

"Then go further into the field," he says, "and you'll find your Virra."

I move off, in a hurry now that I am nearing the end of my journey, but the young bush is too fast for me: "What are you?" he asks.

"I am Wesk. I am a tree."

The rocks and gravel of the ground are hard on my roots, and the surface ice reaches deeper than that in the family, but I hurry on, using the abundant energy of the sun in open air. There are harsh winds out here, too, and they stir my leaves though I try to hold each to the sun.

"A tree?" says the young bush. "Do trees walk?"

Impudence! I say with calm hauteur, "Trees are the world's nobility; we do whatever we wish." I continue away from this ignorant creature, but my roots are tired and sore again from the hard ground. The bush moves after me, and I am startled by his agility.

"Are you really a tree?" he asks. "Yes, you must be — you're so *big!* Are you older than the rocks?"

I try to ignore him, striding on in silence. I notice with a touch of pride that the back-trail where my roots have sunk into the ground is deep and definite, the sign of a giant stalking the earth.

The bush moves in front of me and stops. *"Are* you? Are you older than rocks?"

"Rocks are not people," I say shortly, altering my course to move around him. "Rocks are dead things."

He laughs suddenly, his ridiculous tiny leaves shaking. "Then *they* are older! Everyone knows the old things are dead, and only the younger ones still living." He studies me critically as I begin to step around him. "But you move so slowly! Are you sick, or do all trees move like invalids?"

Anger courses through me; my leaves quiver and I reach out with my longest limbs to cover him with shade. "Go away."

He does not seem to mind, and I notice that he too, like the Virra I seek, can hold the sun in his leaves. He even turns to follow me as I pass.

"Old creatures are ill-tempered, too," he says. "I've heard that the really ancient people, the wonderful meat creatures, were so dissatisfied with the world that they lifted their roots — if they had roots — and flew into the clouds." He giggles. "But when the clouds were gone, so were they."

"I am not a meat creature. Some of them went away, as you say, but those who remained either died or became trees. So you see which of us is the more wonderful: they became us."

I am stepping more rapidly now, as the noon sun softens the ground, but I am still not fast enough to escape this bush. He moves once again, and stands before me.

"You're bad to say such things about the meat creatures. They were so very wonderful; they moved like winter winds and thought great thoughts. You mustn't say bad things about them!"

"Let me pass!" I rumble, stirring the ground so violently with my roots that the bush is pushed backward. I am furious; I reach deliberately for his roots, seize one, and hold him still with my greater strength. I move in on him, intending to drop my limbs around him till he is forced into sleep.

But he does an unthinkable thing: he pulls away from his trapped root, deliberately breaking it off as he scurries back beyond my reach. He stops in the sun, slightly uphill from me, and I see his limbs trembling. (Limbs! They are hardly more than twigs!)

We stare at each other for long minutes, until he says, "All right then, go away. You bore me anyway with your slowness."

I regard him a little while longer, wondering if I can somehow reach him before he escapes again. But he would feel my massive roots pushing toward him underground, and in any case my anger is fading: he is, after all, only an ill-mannered child. Without further word I move on, sinking my roots deep through the surface of ice, drinking what sustenance there is in this rocky soil. My bleeding roots ache but I pay no mind, retaining my dignity. Before night comes, he is out of sight behind me.

I choose this night for sleep. It has been days since I rested, and without the surrounding protection of my family I am chilled by the winds of the field. Besides, bushes are so small: I might walk right past Virra in the dark without seeing her.

In the morning, when the dim rays of the sun touch my highest leaves, I wake refreshed, though my roots seem afire with pain when I free them from the ice and resume walking. The pain passes into a dull ache; I walk till the sun touches my naked trunk, and then I notice that I am being followed.

No, I am being chased. It is a bush, larger than the one I met yesterday, and female. She is lovely, holding her tiny leaves proudly in the morning breeze, stepping delicately past my deeply dug path. In minutes she overtakes me, for I have paused to wait for her. She settles lightly into the ground near me but not in my shade; I study her.

Her leaves are the color and shape I remember; her branches quiver with controlled excitement, just as Virra's did. The light in her leaves is glorious, each a miniature green sun.

"My name is Virra," she says. "Were you looking for me?"

Her voice in my mind is both familiar and strange. Have I forgotten how she sounded, or has she changed since I saw her among the family? Time must pass more quickly for these swiftly moving creatures, after all.

"I believe I have been searching for you since I was born," I say. "But I did not know it until I saw you."

She laughs, and her rustling leaves make music. "But you're a tree. You must be so *old!*"

"No, I have only fifteen rings."

"Fifteen?" Again her rustling laughter. "Then you've lived twice as long as I have. How could you have been looking for me before I was born?"

My blood pulses through me; I feel giddy. "I suppose I believed in you before I ever saw you."

Her leaves are still for a moment. She says in a strangely subdued tone, "Do trees foresee the future, then?"

"No, but we dream. We have time to think, and there are not so many things in the world to think about. So I think of things that do not exist."

"These are dreams?"

"Waking dreams. I think of things I would wish to exist — people filled with light and joy, like you." I pause, embarrassed.

But she does not seem to resent my familiarity; instead, she lifts her leaves to the sun and turns before me, preening. "Am I as beautiful as you dreamed?"

"Even more beautiful. I could never imagine the way you move, so lightly and surely. You amaze me."

She laughs, and the sound is like light rain in my highest branches. "You're silly," she says. "Are all the trees like you?— No, they can't be; the trees I've seen wouldn't even talk to me."

"My family considers me irresponsible," I admit. "I see you agree with them."

"No!" She stops moving and stands before me sedately now. I see her delicate roots sink into the ground, taking sure purchase. "I think you're wonderful. To be able to think of things you've never seen! How fascinating your conversations with your family must be!"

"Alas, no. None of the others ever talk to me of dreams. They tell me to think only of what is real — if not now, then in the past." I sigh, remembering how stern my elders have been with me. "They talk so often of things past.... These are their dreams, but they are not mine."

"Then your dreams are more real than theirs," she says, amused. "You dreamed of me, and here I am."

"Yes, here you are." I am suffused by joy as I realize that I really have found her, at last we are together. The winds of the open field stir my leaves and the ground at my roots seems to shift. — No, it is not the ground that moves: Virra has extended a slender root to touch one of mine. Her touch is as gentle as a caress; hesitantly I reach toward her.

Abruptly she grasps my root and tugs sharply. I recoil, startled rather than hurt, and her root slips away. She backs off quickly, and her laughter rustles softly.

"You're so strong! I've never touched a tree before, but I should have known you'd be strong!"

I am confused by her sudden shift of mood. "Are you mocking me?"

"Oh, no! I'm so tiny beside you, I wouldn't dare! Anyway, you're wonderful and wise, and I'm sure you're gentle, just from seeing how you walk — so calm and dignified. How could I mock you?"

She holds her limbs still as she speaks, as though I were an elder of her family. I feel oddly uncomfortable at this.

"I am simply a tree," I say. "We are a proud family, but I see wonders in you that are new to me. My family descended from the meat people, but yours must have too. No doubt they were different kinds of people who chose to become trees or bushes, but our heritage is the same.... I try to resist my family's pride; please do not tempt me with adulation."

(Yet I remember my scornful rebuke of the ill-mannered bush yesterday. Is this modesty any more appropriate?)

My thoughts are interrupted by another tweaking of my roots: Virra has moved underground again to grasp and jerk at me. She dances lightly away before I can react, and now her laughter is a brook.

"But you're so *serious!*" she cries. "Don't you know you mustn't be serious with bushes?" She pauses. "Have you a name?"

My roots stir the rocks beneath me, but I mutter, "Wesk."

"You're named Wesk? Then please don't be so gloomy, Wesk; you're not in the forest now, you're in the sunlight! Be happy with me — oh, please!"

There is such a note of appeal in her voice that I must respond, confused and doubtful as I am. "What should I do?"

"Play with me!" She begins to dance around me, her roots scarcely touching the icy ground; I think of acorns bouncing down a hillside. I look at her in wonder: this is how the swift meat people must have moved when the sun was young.

(I hear Querca's voice in memory: "They waste the sun, but bushes have no care for that.")

"What shall I do?" I ask.

She continues to circle me. "Do you think you can catch me?"

"No, I could never catch you." I recall yesterday's young bush. "And if I could catch you, I could not hold you."

She edges in closer to me; she is actually standing partly in my shade now. "But you're so clever, Wesk. You know so much. Are you trying to trick me? I know you trees have thoughts so deep they could penetrate boulders."

"Hardly," I say, but I take her cue and stealthily lower my limbs as she advances toward me. She is completely inside my shade now, and perhaps I can trap her before she can retreat. "You are flattering me again, Virra. If you really thought me so wise, you would not challenge my mind."

She continues moving forward, stepping lightly over my roots; I hold them still so that she will not try to flee yet. I continue to lower my limbs, and now they are nearing the ground. She does not seem to notice, for her voice is unconcerned as she says, "We're only playing, Wesk. It's a game—surely even trees play games."

"No, never. I was taught to be serious about all things."

My branches are fully lowered now, my leaves lying flat on the ground behind her. She is trapped; she could never force her way through.

"Then I can teach you about games!" she cries, and suddenly she sprints forward, barely touching the base of my roots as she passes my trunk, her bright leaves brushing against me. She dashes on toward the edge of my shade on the other side, and though I lower the rest of my limbs as quickly as I can, she gains the sun before I can catch her.

She stands quivering as my limbs belatedly strike the

ground, my branches and leaves crashing into the grass. I let them rest there as she begins to giggle. I am mortified to have been tricked so easily.

By the time I have lifted my limbs again, I have recovered some composure. Virra has ceased her laughter, but she dances back and forth in delight. I say, "You *were* mocking me, I see."

"No no, oh no! You *are* clever or you could never have thought of trapping me that way when you've never played a game before! But I'm used to games, you know; so I realized what you might do."

"You are clever too, Virra, though you pretended you were not."

She notices the ruefulness in my voice, for she says quickly, "We each played tricks, but I started mine first — it was *my* game, after all. Oh, please don't be angry with me. It was a *game.*"

"Games must give more joy to those who are successful at them," I say.

"Well, of *course* it's more fun to win! But it wouldn't be any fun at all if you couldn't lose." She rustles her leaves playfully at me. "I'll bet you trees never take any chances at all. You just sit there in your forest trying to stay alive. What for? It's such a waste!"

I am shaken by her words. She is right: so many of us do nothing but dream of the past while trying to live longer into the future — separating ourselves further from the time of ancient joys. It seems a paradox, yet my entire life's teachings go against what she says.

I notice that she stands directly over my longest root, and cautiously, reaching deeper into the rocky ground of the field, I extend the root until it reaches past her. I am not sure why I continue to play this game; perhaps it is to please her.

Yet I promised Querca that I would question Virra's way of wasting the sun, and if I keep her talking perhaps she will not notice that I am trying to capture her. "You should not accuse me of waste," I say, "for you burn the sun's energy each hour of each day. The sun is dying; you must know that. My family gathers its energy, and if we live for a long time we may preserve the fruit of the sun for centuries after final darkness falls."

This brings leaf-shaking laughter from Virra. "The sun, may be dying, but we'll die much sooner. Does it matter what may happen centuries from now?"

I do not reply immediately; I am raising the tip of my root to the surface. She takes my silence for agreement, and goes on, "You think of the ancient past, days that are dead, and you think of the future, days that may never come. Don't you ever think of *now?*"

There is surprising passion in her speech. While her attention is distracted, I break the icy ground silently with my root and suddenly reach to grasp her slender trunk. At the last moment she sees me reaching for her and tries to spring away, but I grasp and hold her tightly. She writhes in my grip, but I am too strong for her; and she cannot tear away from her main body.

After a minute she subsides, though I continue to hold her fast. In the silence that follows I say, "We are capable of thinking of now. As you see."

Quietly she says, "All right, you've caught me. You *are* clever, Wesk, just as I said. This time you've won; now let me go."

"No. I shall continue to hold you, and in this way I shall remain the victor."

Her body trembles with pent energy; I feel that I am

holding life trapped forever. But abruptly the tension is gone, as she relaxes completely. "You really don't know anything at all about games, do you?" she says. "You can't win just by holding on to something. If you could, you might as well chase rocks."

She says no more. I continue to hold her but she does not try to move. Eventually I loosen my grip and withdraw my root into the cold ground.

I feel suddenly morose. "Then what use is victory? Time eats everything, it seems; the past is a monster that follows us everywhere."

Her voice is gentle: "You're right — our past is enormous, greater than anything in the world. But while we keep moving, it can't reach us."

"Then we can only run away from it." The thought is ice reaching down to my roots.

But again her mood changes. "Oh, no, Wesk, we can move in so many ways that aren't running! Let me show you!"

She begins to dance. I have seen her do it before, the graceful motions of roots and limbs, leaves swaying without wind; when she walked through my forest-family she moved like this. I recognized it as something wonderful then, and perhaps it was this that caused me to follow her so far. She dances in a circle around me and I watch in awe; gradually I begin to notice patterns in her movements, repeated figures, slight dippings of her branches, and even a kind of sound among her leaves that is rustling, but more than that — is she singing with her body?

She returns to the point where she began her dance, and pauses. "You see? I'm back here again, but the past is gone; it's chasing me, but it will never catch up."

My branches feel as though they are swaying, though I can feel that they are still. The winds of the field seem warm.

"You are so lovely," I murmur. "Does beauty hypnotize the past, then?"

"No, it isn't like that. Don't you see, Wesk? Dancing *is* beautiful, if you want to call it that — it's happiness. Can you dance too? Oh, of course you can! Come dance with me, dear Wesk!"

"I cannot. I am too slow."

"You *can*. Be stately, be dignified; it doesn't matter. Just move and be happy. I'll show you."

She begins to dance again, this time in a leisurely, languorous way. Her tiny branches sway gently like those of the great sun-gatherers; her roots caress the frost-crusted soil. I watch her, and her rhythms penetrate to my heart.

Hesitantly I begin to dance too. I make a step toward her, and another step with a different root. The icy ground grips me but I ignore it; I imitate her movements. I feel foolish and clumsy, but joy spreads in me.

"There!" she says. "You see?" She turns a complete circle where she stands, leaving delicate marks where she has touched the ground. "Can you do that?"

I try; jerkily and with great effort I withdraw my roots from the ground and turn. The winds rush through my branches, confusing me because they seem to come from all directions at once. I have to stop then, for I am exhausted and overcome by vertigo; I sink one long root directly down into the soil for strength, hoping she will not notice.

I find that I am laughing. It is an utterly strange feeling, yet delicious. The ground around me trembles and the surface ice cracks in a thousand tiny lines.

"You *can* dance! I knew you could!" Virra's branches raise into the air; the emerald light of her leaves is silhouetted by the deepening red of the late-afternoon sky.

"But not for long," I say faintly.

"Oh, yes! You can dance whenever you want, and for as long as you want!"

She is wrong. I am no bush who can drink surface frost and store sunlight in my leaves. My roots ache and bleed, and I can no longer hold my branches up to the sun. I stand motionless; I am finished, and the winds become cold again.

Virra sees the way my limbs bend, and she ceases her dance. The sun is almost set; I could gather no more energy from it anyway. She moves to me, stepping as lightly as ever past my roots. I sink them into the ground to allow her easier passage, then continue to reach for the warmer earth beneath the surface. Soon I am deeply rooted, and the sun is completely gone, and Virra stands at the very base of my roots, her small branches wrapped around my trunk.

"You're very brave," she says. "I didn't know trees could still be brave."

I feel her roots reaching down into the soil and wrapping around one of mine; they feel warm.

"I can dance," I say in wonder. "Though I know I do it badly."

"You'll get better when you've practiced a while."

The night is freezing cold. "If I do more, it will bring me to death," I tell her.

Her leaves are the only spots of light left. She keeps them wrapped around me and I catch what energy I can from them. Is she deliberately feeding me? My family would call it madness.

"I'd never cause you to die," she says softly.

Exhaustion and cold are sending me inexorably into sleep, but I manage to say, "I love you."

Then I do fall asleep, and I know nothing more till late the next morning, when I wake slowly and raise my limbs to the sun, and move my roots as I begin to loosen the frozen earth, and discover that Virra is gone.

At first I wait patiently for her to return, convinced that she has merely gone off on some unpredictable bush-whim. Perhaps she has; but she does not come back, though I stand rooted and drinking, spreading my limbs and gathering energy to dance again if she wishes. The red disk of the sun reaches zenith and begins to descend; I am anxious now but I remain where she left me. In a way I am grateful to have this time to mend and grow strong again. I remember her laughter, and the way she danced and played with me, and at times it seems I am dreaming.

When the sun sets I lower my limbs, drawing them in as close to me as I can, holding what warmth I have for as long as I can. In the dark, still watching for her, I begin to remember things she said:

Am I as beautiful as you dreamed?... But you're so *serious!* Don't you know you mustn't be serious with bushes?... You can't win just by holding on to something. If you could, you might as well chase rocks.

I watch for the light of her leaves, but she does not come. The night grows colder, and I sleep.

In the morning I wake early, and see a bush nearby. The sun's light is still dim, but I see tiny glowing leaves. "You've come back!" I cry.

"No."

That one word chills me more than ice, for it is not her voice.

"I've never seen you before," the bush says. "What are you doing so far out here? You're a tree!"

Without knowing why, I explode with anger at this... accusation. "Trees own the world! We are the final product of all history, the greatest of creatures!" I tremble so violently that ice shards fall from my limbs and the ground is shattered around me.

The bush moves quickly away from me. "You're as ridiculous as the rest. How did you get here?"

"I walked! Trees can walk—we can even dance. We can do anything!" My blood is rising now, filling my trunk and limbs; it brings pain even as the night frost falls away. I shake my leaves at the bush, though it is not wholly a voluntary act.

The bush laughs at me. It is the size of Virra; it is even female like her. But its laughter holds ridicule. "If you can dance, then show me. Oh, I'd love to see you dance! Will boulders dance next?"

"I dance only for Virra." My voice is as cold as the morning wind.

"*I'm* Virra. Dance for me."

Enraged, I try to leap after the bush, lifting three roots at once from the ground and flailing clumsily. Rocks and wedges of ice fly through the air. The bush retreats further, and I am caught by my remaining roots, which are sunk so deep that I must pause to work them loose.

"Is that what you call dancing?"

I stretch my free roots toward her, but she is too far away. I would grasp and rend her, strip her leaves, smother her with my own, and gather ice from the ground to heap upon her.

"You are *not* Virra! Where is she?" But my voice cannot rumble and threaten as I want: it pleads.

The bush laughs again. "Of course I'm Virra. We're all Virra."

Something touches me that is not frost, but it is cold. The young bush I first met said he was Virra too. "What do you mean?" I ask, still struggling to free my deep-sunk roots.

She stands oddly still, and her voice is softer when she

speaks again. "You don't know, do you? *All* the bushes are called Virra — why should we care about names?"

I am bewildered, though something in me says I should have known this. The bushes live so briefly; they move around so that they have no ground of their own; they hold on to nothing, not even names.

Not even to love. Least of all to loving me.

I force myself to speak: "There was one of you who came to me and gave me joy. But she went away, and I have to find her."

The winds of the field continue to rush by us. The bush asks, "How long ago?"

"Two days. Less."

The emerald glow of this person's leaves is as bright as Virra's — the real Virra's. "Then you'll never catch up to her."

Even the voice of this Virra sounds like hers now. It is an unreal world here in the great open field; nothing is as it should be.

I have at least freed my remaining roots — I can walk now, but I do not know in which direction to search. Confused and fearful, I look for the tiny root-tracks Virra must have left. But the ground is covered with frost.

Hopelessly I say, "You must know where Virra went. Tell me."

"How could I know? I don't even know which Virra you mean; we're alike to each other." She hesitates, seeing my leaves shake. "Anyway, she must have gone so far by now that you'll never find her."

"I *will!*" The force of my cry frightens the bush, and she runs. In minutes she has disappeared over a low hillock. I watch her disappearance as though she were hope itself, for I realize that she is right: I could never overtake Virra even if I knew in what direction to go.

I hold my limbs up to the chill sun and consider my situation. I have only two chances: either Virra will return to this spot, or I must hope to find her by a blind search of the field. Neither possibility seems likely, but I must do something. So I begin.

I walk through windy fields strewn with rocks and chunks of ice. I search for Virra while the dim red sun rises and sets, rises and sets more times than I bother to count. I have no direction; I turn to left or right when hopelessness strikes me, and I continue though all I find are the mindless grasses, and rocks and empty ground, and occasionally a traveling bush.

"I search for one called Virra. Are you Virra?"

"We're all Virra."

I go on, hopeless but hoping.

Several times I return to the place where I stood when Virra left. But she is never there, and there are never any tracks except my own deep root-holes. Each time I think: She will see them if she comes, and she will be able to find me.

But she never does, and though the memory of trees is greater than that of any other beings who have lived, I am beginning to forget what Virra was like. Bright green in her leaves, yes, but precisely what color? Her laughter rustled with life, but what was its sound?

One thing I do remember clearly. The last words Virra said to me were, "I'd never cause you to die." I believed it was a statement of love, but it must have been something else.

It was high summer when I left my family, but I can feel the ground growing cold at deeper levels as the sun dims toward winter. Walking is harder each day, yet I continue. My roots have become tough, lacerated by stones but covered now with something that is almost bark. I move ever more slowly.

One day I find myself at the edge of the forest-family. The hermits stand silent and I do not disturb them; perhaps they are already in their winter sleep. Beyond them is darkness, and the warmth of hundreds of my family huddled together. I recall how the ground moves within the family, stirred constantly by our roots.

I look once more at the great empty field, filled with winds and strangers. My soul is utterly silent as I step carefully into the shade of an unmoving hermit, skirt her roots, and move on into the forest. I step painfully from one patch of sun to another; the trees grow more numerous and closer together, and after a while I begin to hear their vague dreams, but I ignore them.

Then a voice comes: "Well. Did you find her?"

It is Querca, who promised she would remember me when I came again. Aged and great Querca, who once filled me with fear. Now I feel nothing.

"Yes, I found her."

Querca's brittle leaves rustle. "A creature who kills the sun. How did she explain that?"

I stop and sink my roots deep; deliberately I drink the soil that Querca has owned since before I was born. Querca is too old to object, or perhaps it is the coming of winter that keeps her still.

"She said the sun's energy is for life, and for joy. She said we waste it if we do not use it." I feel Querca's contempt stir the ground, but before she can speak I add, "I believe she is right."

"Then why are you returning?"

There is no way to explain what happened. "I lost her," I say.

"I see. Of course."

There is silence, as there usually is in the family during

winter. Finally Querca asks, "How was the soil there? Rich and soft, as it is here?"

Her words cause me to move my roots in the deep loam of the family. "There were rocks. The soil everywhere was dry beneath the ice."

"As bad as I thought," says Querca. "They will not remain much longer."

"But while they remain, they *live!*"

Querca suppresses laughter in her roots before it can reach her leaves and cause them to fall. "When the end comes, there will be no bushes left," she says. "We shall inherit all."

Suddenly I am flooded by emotion, and it takes me several minutes to realize what it is: I feel pity for Querca.

I withdraw my roots from her soil and turn toward the field. Stepping carefully away, I say, "Then let the end come."

And now I am walking again toward the edge of the family. I shall find a place outside the forest, beyond the hermits and perhaps touching the stones of the field. If Virra — any Virra — comes to me, I will try to dance again.

# NIGHT OF THE LIVING OLDPHARTS

As they rounded the turn in the road they came out of the shade of oak and elm trees and started up a low hill. Jimmy accelerated through the open fields on either side, excited now that they were actually coming to their new home. The building stood on a ridge to the right, off a short unpaved driveway; the VW van's tires sent up dust the color of Buff Copier Paper #2 as they approached the building on the crest of the rise.

Juleen stared ahead with fascination. "Is that it?" she asked. "Wow, it must've been a great con hotel—looks like it couldn't have held more than a couple of hundred people, even counting the fans who slept on the floor in sleeping bags."

"About a third of them did that," said Jimmy. "Wimpycon never drew many people on expense accounts. Even the pros at those conventions were people who'd only sold stories to *Fantasy Book* or maybe a novel to Starblaze."

The driveway curled to a stop in front of the hotel and Jimmy shut off the van's engine; they sat there looking at the building's three-story front while the engine cooled, giving off slow ticking noises like a Geiger counter in Heinlein's basement.

"It's beautiful," Juleen said. "I don't think we're going to need all the space even when our book and fanzine collections get here."

Jimmy nodded. "But science fiction fans have to look to the future. Who knows, maybe everybody in fandom will start publishing monthly like they used to do. There are so many oldpharts coming back into fandom these days, and they don't know much about fannish progress..."

"Progress indeed," said Juleen as she opened her door and climbed out. Jimmy got out too; he went around the front of the van and put an arm around Juleen's waist. They leaned their heads together as they looked at the deserted building. Memories came to Jimmy of the conventions he'd attended here when it had been a hotel and everything had been alive, the con members wearing beanies instead of Spock ears: truly alive. Wimpycon had been the last of the real fannish conventions, probably because it had been out here away from the urban centers of blight and walk-in attendees. He conjured up images of Bill Bowers and Dave Locke, Martha Beck and Bob Tucker, all of the last of the old crowd.

They began to bustle around the back of the van, unloading their first bunch of belongings: the most important ones, the bedclothes and kitchen utensils, their plates and glasses and their copier. Jimmy set this out on top of a stack of blankets, and Juleen said, "Will you finally tell me how we got this incredibly big house? I still don't believe it's ours. What's the secret?"

"Thank the federal government," said Jimmy as he carefully brought out his word processor. "The local fanclub bought the building several years ago so they could hold conventions here, but then the IRS decided that cons weren't really non-profit so they demanded back taxes from just about every con committee in the country, and the Wimpycon organizers got caught in that. They tried to explain that the biggest profit anyone at any of their cons had had was when Howard DeVore sold a copy of Harlan Ellison's *Science Fantasy Bulletin* for ten dollars, but the IRS people didn't believe it. They attached Wimpycon's holdings and put everything up at auction; that was why I managed to buy their con hotel so cheap. I mean, who'd buy this big building out in the middle of nowhere? Nobody but a faaan."

"That's why I love you," Juleen said. "You're a fan but you aren't stupid; you almost restore my faith in fandom."

They'd finished unloading the van by nightfall, placing box after box in the first-floor rooms, except for the bedding, which they carried up to the SMOF Suite on the third floor. (It had been the Governor's Suite in the years when this had been a commercial hotel, but the fans had replaced the sign when they'd bought the building.) The room had a view to the west, so they moved chairs to the window and sat watching the sun go down at the far horizon; the sky was a melange of red and gold, like a Powers cover without the lettering.

Jimmy ruffled the back of his bride's hair and said, "So now we're the owners of a home where we can hold conventions of our own. Maybe we'd better get busy making new little gofers to help us out."

Juleen smiled and shrugged away from his hand. "We haven't even made up the bed yet. Anyway, who says I want to hold cons here? I think we should just invite a bunch of fans whenever we have a fanzine to assemble."

"Two hundred fans just for an assembly session?" Jimmy

said. "They'd all take their own copies and we wouldn't have any left to send out."

"So who needs to send fanzines to the east and west coasts?" Juleen wrinkled her nose. "Think wimpy, love. If Ben Yalow wants a copy he can come and assemble one."

"What's that out there?" Jimmy broke in. He pointed to a shadowed area in the fields. Juleen looked, but apparently didn't see anything.

"It's nothing," she said. "Looks like Michael Ashley's soul."

But there was some kind of movement out there, and soon she saw it too; she drew in a breath. Was it cows coming in for the night? A truck on the highway? No; there were no lights. "Maybe it's a couple of teenagers wandering around looking for a place to spoon," she said uncertainly.

Jimmy looked a while longer but saw nothing more. He shrugged. "Probably just a trick of the light. Let's go downstairs and see if that big old kitchen still works."

Juleen cast a final glance out into the fields, then followed him out of the suite and down the stairs. They went into the now needlessly large kitchen and began to set out the makings for dinner. They'd brought only a few days' supply of food, but there were a couple of steaks that had thawed during their long drive from Cleveland; the kitchen had a microwave oven, so dinner was soon ready. They carried plates full of steaks and salad out to the dining room and turned on the artificial fireplace next to the table they chose. Jimmy began to eat, thinking of Tanith Lee stories: so much new technology just to recreate the details of a nontechnological past.

"Sorry if I scared you upstairs," he said. "For a minute I really did think I'd seen something out in the fields."

"Never mind, love. Remember, I read science fiction, not

fantasy. If you'd married someone who grew up reading Stephen King stories it'd be different."

Suddenly they heard low voices outside, then the sound of breaking glass. Jimmy saw everything over Juleen's shoulder: three of the west windows being smashed in; tall, hulking figures, indistinct in the growing dark, coming in through them. They moved jerkily and uncertainly, like people Jack Speer might have drawn.

Juleen gasped and rose from her chair; she said, "Is this some kind of joke?"

The creatures were human, but they seemed to be sniffing as they advanced across the dining room and their heads moved left and right as they came on, brushing aside tables and chairs. Jimmy stared in wonder and fright: the creatures seemed enormous, taller than James White, dire and dreadful. But there was a lambent light in their eyes that made them seem almost ... fannish.

Then he noticed the beanies.

They all wore them, but they were covered with dust and mud, the propellors bent and cracked; despite the wind that blew in through the smashed windows, none of the propellors turned. It gave the creatures a forlorn, tragic appearance, and now Jimmy saw that all of them were smiling — frightening rictus grins of the gafiated and damned. He felt sorry for them even as goosebumps prickled all over his body.

Juleen didn't scream; she'd been nurtured on the stories of Tiptree and Russ, so she stood and faced them. She was trembling, but she was ready to stand against them; seeing that, Jimmy too stood up.

The creatures mumbled and muttered as they came on; Jimmy couldn't make out what they were saying till the first one came near. It stopped a few feet from them, its face

muscles twitching like those of someone who had just lost a
Hugo to Dick Geis, and it raised a hand. Its fellows moved
jerkily to its side, and then one of them said in a voice as
faded as hektographed fanzines:

"Let's put out oneshot."

Jimmy and Juleen watched in horrified fascination as the
strange beings set up an ancient mimeograph on one of
the tables, and on several others, ancient typewriters. The
creatures spoke among themselves in low voices that seemed
to emanate from beneath the ground, and fetid odors of the
past enveloped Jimmy as he saw that the mimeograph wasn't
even a Gestetner; it was something primordial, a Roneo or
an A. B. Dick, open-drummed and creaking as one of the
beings cranked it with a palsied hand to shake out the dust
and cobwebs.

And the typewriters, the typewriters! They weren't even
electric; they were ancient Remingtons and Royals, manual
machines whose keys wouldn't move when someone touched
them; you had to *strike* them. The dreadful beings rolled
blue stencils into their typewriters, stencils they'd brought in
quires *(quires?)* that had never been opened, and the large
dining room was filled with a minty smell that evoked
memories of long-gafiated demons. (Claude Degler? thought
Jimmy. George Wetzel?)

"Oneshot, oneshot," chanted the huge creatures as they
went about their tasks, and Jimmy wandered among them,
more curious than afraid now that he'd seen what they
were: ancient fans returned, the oldpharts of his childhood
nightmares, the objects of his adolescent fury.

"The nametags," Juleen said softly. "Do you see their
nametags?"

"Yes," Jimmy said. "Yes, I see them." The creatures

wore badges from conventions decades in the past, multiple fandoms ago; they even had drawings on them by Bjo, Ray Nelson, and other fanartists of the ancient days.

"But I've never heard of these fans," Juleen said. "They're not even fans from the *south*."

Indeed they weren't. Jimmy read the names but seldom recognized them. Bob Lichtman? Mal Ashworth? Art Rapp? Arthur Thomson? Chuch Harris? Who were they, these twitching and shambling revenants from times before *Dr. Who* and even *Star Trek*? He peered at more nametags: Vinc Clarke, Lenny Bailes, Wrai Ballard... The names seemed to strike a chord in Jimmy's memory, somewhere deep where he'd buried them many years ago. He couldn't repress a shudder now: it was as though Lovecraft's Elder Gods had returned to Earth, to this onetime conhotel that had been built long after their time. He thought for a moment that he heard one of them say, "Ia! Ia! Shub Niggurath!"—but no, the creature had only been clearing its rheumy throat.

And now he saw a truly horrifying sight. One of the beings opened a tattered paper bag and brought forth strange, arcane implements: after a frozen, breathless time Jimmy realized what they were. Lettering guides, he thought, and writing plates and styluses and shading plates. The creature bent over a stencil and began to draw on it; then, with quick, precise movements, it brought into play one of the lettering guides and inscribed a title.

OMEGA: THE ULTIMATE FANZINE, it said.

The ancient oldphart looked up at Jimmy when it had finished. It waved a hand shakily at him, and with a voice as weak as the ConStellation financial records it mumbled, "You... write now. Do fanac!"

It thrust a blank stencil at him and Jimmy took it, holding it fearfully between finger and thumb. The stencil shook in his hand and seemed to curl up to grasp his wrist. Jimmy looked to his wife in awe and fright.

"Do it," she whispered. "You've got to write something, or they'll — " She shuddered. "Or they'll call you a fakefan."

He didn't want that. Though the term was ancient, he knew it for the curse it was: it could turn him into an apahack, or something worse. Jimmy looked at the stencil, then put it down on a table and went to get his word processor from one of the boxes they'd brought in earlier.

He set it carefully on a table and plugged it in. Immediately the lights in the dining room went out and they were plunged into darkness, surrounded by the frightening oldpharts. He heard them cry out in anger: "Fout! Foutfout*fout*! Neofans! *Sci-fi fans!*" Their voices were suddenly clear and strong.

"...probably read trilogies..." one of them said.

Several of the creatures lit candles, and others switched on flashlights. Jimmy heard one of them mutter, "...used to keep one in bed...read stefmags under the covers..." and in the dimness all around the room others nodded. The ancient machines began to type again.

But his word processor couldn't work without electricity. He looked to Juleen at her own word processor, and saw her stand up and move to a table where a battered typewriter sat. He went to stand behind her and saw her type heavily onto a stencil, "I am a fan, though I'm not sure why..."

Several of the oldphart revenants were watching too. In mumbling, muttering tones one of them said, "...good. Good first sentence. Write more." And Juleen continued to type, striking typewriter keys that hadn't moved since...when? Since Sixth Fandom? Or earlier?

Two of the creatures converged on Jimmy, grasped his arms and led him to another table where a dust-covered typewriter sat. One of them rolled a stencil into it and the other pushed Jimmy down into a chair. "You write," the being said. "Pub ish!"

Jimmy stared fearfully at the blank stencil, and memories came to him of the time he'd had to produce activity requirements for Apa 65. He'd been up till nearly dawn then and had just barely gotten his fanzine done in time. But he hadn't had to contend with stencils that time, nor a clumsy antique typewriter...

"Write!" said the creature again, and Jimmy put his fingers to the keyboard. The machine lay dead before him: no hum inside it, not the slightest vibration in the keys. How could anyone have produced fanzines on such a device? He thought desperately and something came to him; he typed:

Once uon amidnigt fanis,

While I typd thigs ingroup ,clannsh

He was having great trouble making the keys strike. The gray oldphart behind him grasped his hands and drew them away from the keyboard, then handed him a small bottle labeled *Correction Fluid.* The being pointed shakily at his stencil and said, "Fix!" Its voice seemed to emanate from the nether depths of Puerto Rico.

Jimmy opened the bottle of correction fluid and smeared some of it on the lines he'd typed so badly. He put his fingers back on the typewriter keys, but the oldphart said, "Wait. Wait for dry." Jimmy waited long minutes till the creature nudged him and said, "Now fix," then laboriously he typed the lines again; he got them right this time. The creatures's faded voice said, "Now go on."

The interruption had broken Jimmy's train of concentration; he sat looking at his stencil without an idea in his head. All around him he heard the clatter of fan revenants typing, sending a massive noise up to the Lord. (Probably Roscoe, Jimmy thought, and grimaced.) They muttered to themselves as they struck the keys: "Fifty dominoes, that's not too many," and "I had one grunch, but it stole Christmas," and "The ship developed a list to port, which was quickly corrected to chablis."

The dusty revenant behind him said, "You *write!*" So Jimmy found more words in his head, and he laboriously typed:

About many a thing from fanzines

Concerning forgotten lore

The revivified being behind him grasped his hands again, and said in its faded voice, "...not scan." It handed him the bottle of correction fluid. "Write again."

So Jimmy rewrote the lines:

Of the many things that happened

In forgotten fannish lore

And this time the oldphart made no objection. It merely said, "...standards. Standards of quality. No typoes, no misspellings, no errors...at all..."

Jimmy was tired, and looking across the room at Juleen he saw that she too was showing the strains of exhaustion. She could now hardly strike the typewriter keys correctly. One of the gray ancients passed behind her and stopped; it pointed a shaking finger and said, "Typo! Typo! You fix!" And it thrust another tiny bottle of correction fluid at her.

"Ted White makes typos!" she protested, but the oldphart made her take the bottle and correct half a line.

"Ted White edits comic books," the creature muttered.

And so it went for hours. The ancient revenants typed rapidly on their stencils, and when one finished an article or story it stood up and gave its stencils to the oldphart seated before the — Jimmy searched his memory for the word — the mimeoscope, and that creature lettered a title and an illustration. Meanwhile another of the ancients sat down before the vacated typewriter and began to write its own contribution to the oneshot.

At last, shortly before morning, Jimmy finished the piece he'd been writing. Juleen had finished hers a few minutes before, and suddenly Jimmy realized that all the other typewriters had stopped clattering too. He sank back into his chair, thankful that his work was over — but the oldpharts gave him no rest. One of them herded him to a corner of the room where he saw with dismal recognition the ancient mimeograph. The revenants had been cranking it for over an hour now but Jimmy, involved in writing, had paid little attention.

"Run off...last two pieces," muttered one of the gray creatures. "She collate...we make addresses on...mailing wrapper."

Just like that, Jimmy was forced to deal with a mimeograph. He had seldom even seen such a thing; he had never had to run one. But one of the oldpharts put a stencil on its drum and adjusted the inking, and then one of them clumsily punched his shoulder and he had to stand there cranking out copies by hand. Many times the paper feed crumpled a sheet in the workings of the machine and one of the revenants had to extricate it for him; twice the ink ran too low and they replenished it. He lost track of the number of copies he'd run off, but the oldpharts counted the good copies and told him how many more he had to run. Did they really do this all the time, back then? Jimmy wondered to himself; but he kept on cranking and the sheets piled up.

Eventually he was finished. He fell into a chair and watched numbly as Juleen collated the last few pages and stapled the completed fanzines. The revenants wrote names and addresses on the mailing wrappers, consulting a mailing list that Jimmy recognized as the one rich brown kept continually updated. (The fact that they had that list confirmed what Jimmy had always thought of rich brown.) Then other revenants put stamps on the mailing wrappers, crying out in their own horror as they studied a manual on the latest postal rates.

Finally the ordeal was over. The dread gray oldpharts smiled their rictus smiles and one of them said, "Tomorrow you mail." It looked around and realized that the room was lit not only by candles and flashlights but also by the morning sun. *"Today* you mail," said the creature, and then they all shambled away through the broken windows. Jimmy and Juleen watched as they went through the fields outside; in the early-morning shadows their hulking figures disappeared like audiences at fan-panels.

The following year, when the Worldcon was in Norway and Jimmy and Juleen couldn't afford to attend, they got a phone call. One of their friends said, "Hey, you won the Hugo Award for Best Fanzine! At least I guess you won it, because *Omega* was the winner and you're the only fans I know who were involved in it. *Omega* got so many votes that the committee waived the rule against oneshots."

Jimmy and Juleen had a huge party the next night with over a hundred fans present, but they dodged every question about how they'd gotten so many of the fans of the past to contribute. They were pleased; they were happy about the award; but somehow they were afraid too.

A week later the new windows of their dining room were smashed, and the oldpharts came back. "Another oneshot!" they shouted. "We pub ish . . . every year!"

And Jimmy suddenly understood fandom.